Friends

BEYOND

MEASURE

Friends
BEYOND
MEASURE

Lalena Fisher

HARPER

An Imprint of HarperCollinsPublishers

COPYRIGHT

Title	Friends Beyond Measure
Author	Copyright © 2023 by Lalena Fisher
Legal Language	All Rights Reserved. Manufactured in Italy. No part of this book may be used or reproduced in any manner whatsoever without written permission except in the case of brief quotations embodied in critical articles and reviews. For information address HarperCollins Children's Books, a division of HarperCollins Publishers, 195 Broadway, New York NY 10007 · www.harpercollinschildrens.com
International Standard Book Number	978-0-06-321052-3
Art Media	The illustrations in this book were created with pencil, marker, and Adobe Photoshop.
Book Designer	Chelsea C. Donaldson
Mysterious Numbers	24 25 26 RTLO 10 9 8 7 6 5 4 3
Edition	First edition

DEDICATION: For Shelley Ann Jackson

- ✓ Jokester
- ✓ Educator
- ✓ Author-Illustrator
- ✓ Mom
- ✓ Friend Extraordinaire

ME   BOTH   YOU

It started the day we met.

ME   YOU

I thought the fun would last forever!

After all, we had played

for hours and hours!

You were so good at a lot of stuff.

And I was good at other stuff.

We had adventures!

15

We had disagreements . . .

and then agreements.

NUMBER OF CHICKENS WHO LEARNED TO FLY WHILE ON THE MOON: 9 out of 10

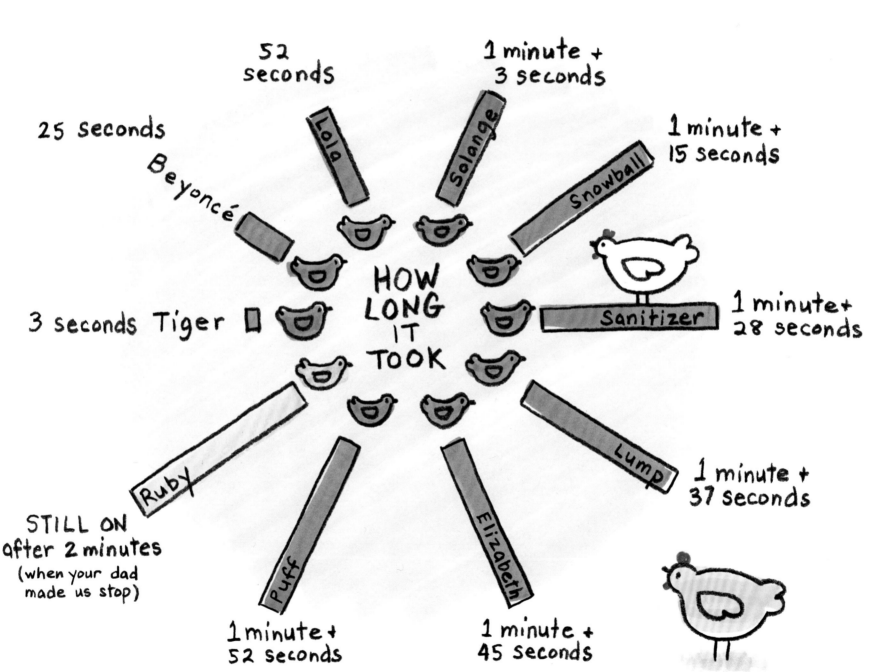

52 seconds — Lola

1 minute + 3 seconds — Solange

25 seconds — Beyoncé

1 minute + 15 seconds — Snowball

3 seconds — Tiger

1 minute + 28 seconds — Sanitizer

HOW LONG IT TOOK

STILL ON after 2 minutes (when your dad made us stop) — Ruby

1 minute + 52 seconds — Puff

1 minute + 45 seconds — Elizabeth

1 minute + 37 seconds — Lump

You told me you were moving.

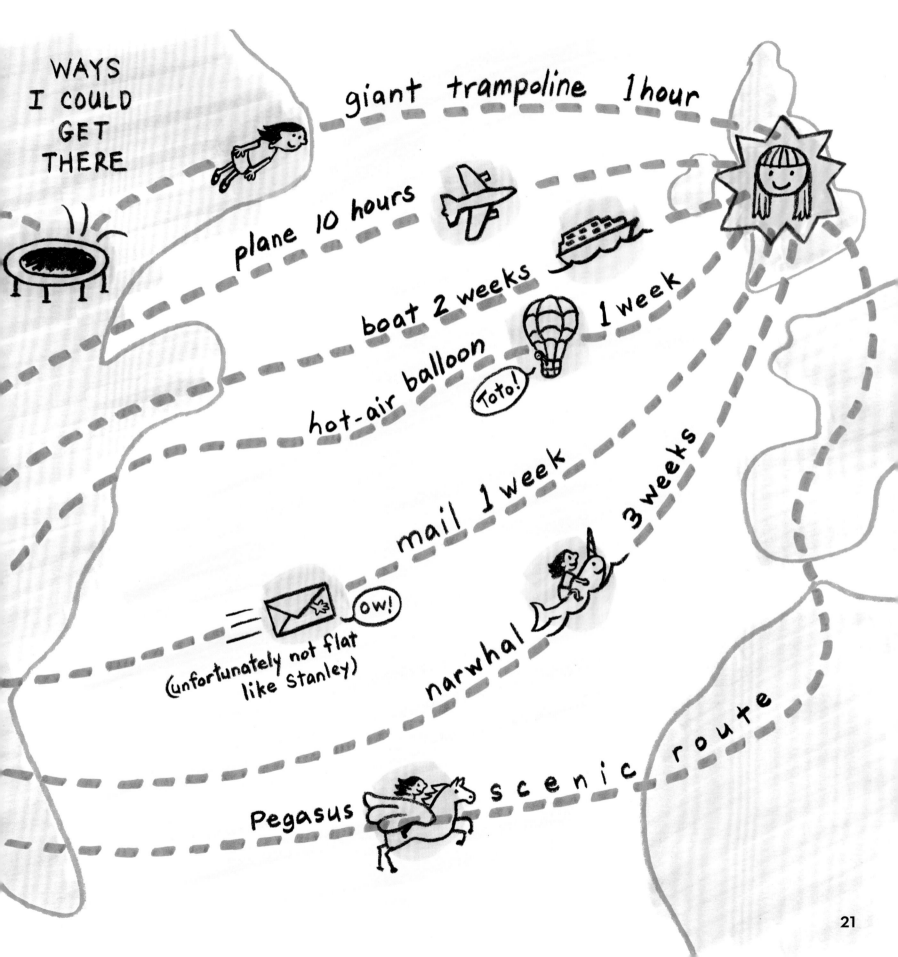

WAYS I COULD GET THERE

giant trampoline 1 hour

plane 10 hours

boat 2 weeks

hot-air balloon 1 week

Toto!

mail 1 week

(unfortunately not flat like Stanley)

ow!

narwhal 3 weeks

Pegasus scenic route

I'll go to a horse camp there.

SADNESS

EXCITEMENT for you

22

I had so many feelings.

After that, no matter how I sliced it,

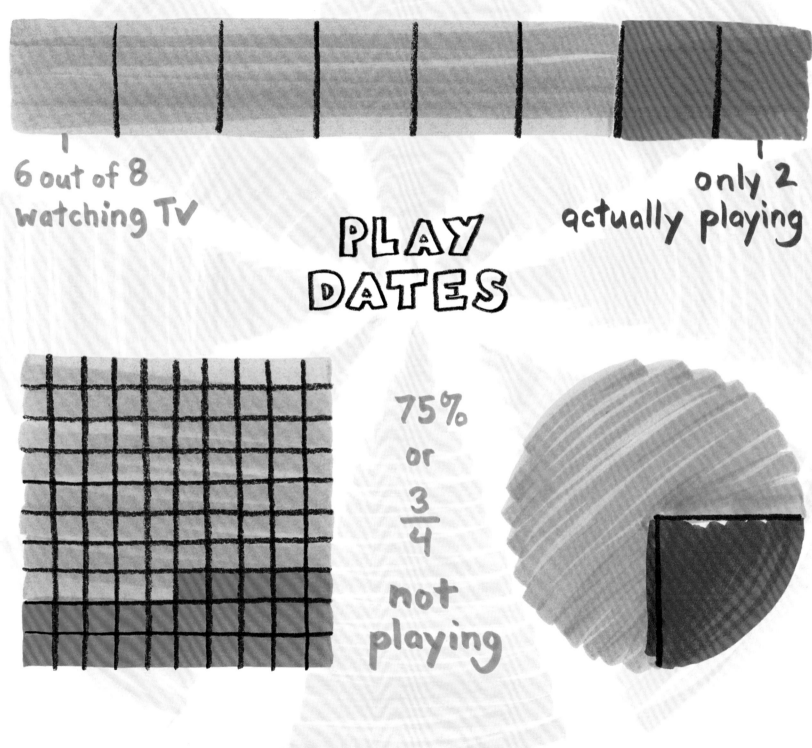

6 out of 8
watching TV

only 2
actually playing

PLAY
DATES

75%
or
$\frac{3}{4}$
not
playing

things were different.

And time was passing fast!

What could I do?

Pack myself in your suitcase?

HMMM...

YES
if

Do I like
the dark?

if
NO

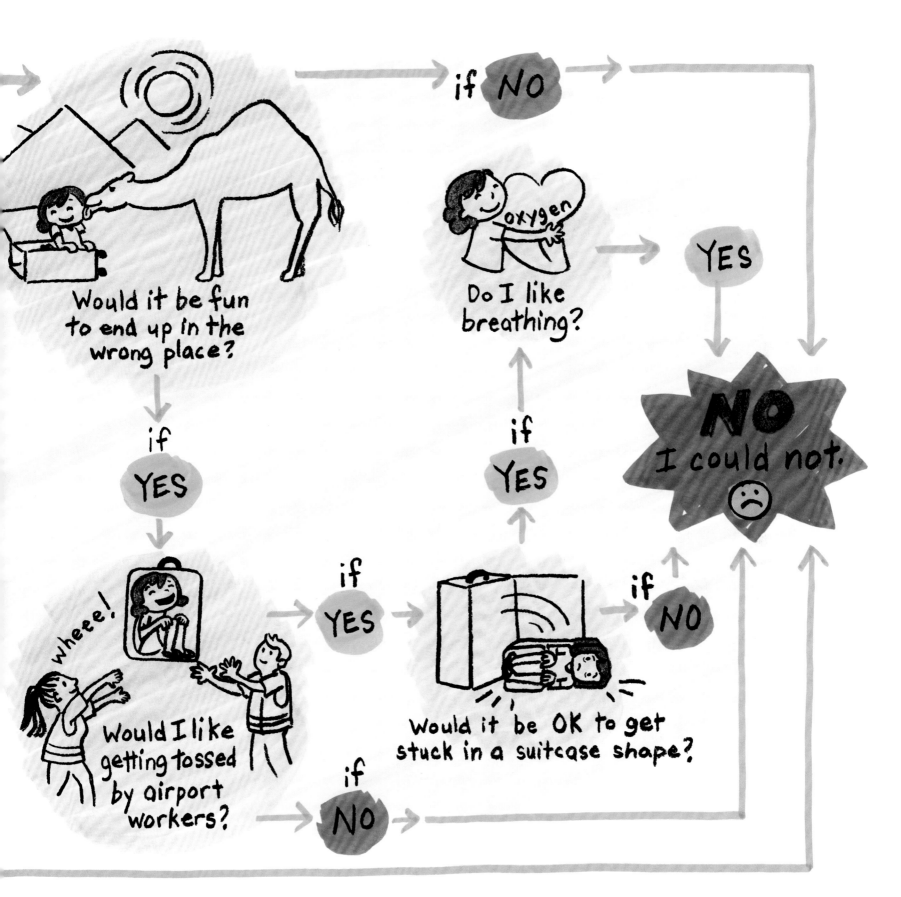

if NO

Would it be fun to end up in the wrong place?

Do I like breathing?

oxygen

YES

if YES

if YES

NO
I could not.

wheee!

Would I like getting tossed by airport workers?

if YES

Would it be OK to get stuck in a suitcase shape?

if NO

if NO

KITCHEN STUFF
- COOKWARE
- DISHES
- GADGETS

OTHER STUFF
- KNICKKNACKS
- TCHOTCHKES
- BRIC-A-BRAC

CLOTHES
- SHIRTS
- SKIRTS
- PANTS
- HATS
- COSTUMES
- SHOES
- PAJAMAS

TOYS
- babies
- DOLLS
- animals
- board games
- puzzles
- GAMES
- CREATIVE
- plush — HORSES
- plastic
- wood

I didn't want you to leave.

We will *always* be friends.

This year,

Letters

Messages

Calls

34

next year . . .

Trade fairy tea recipes

Make a book together

Virtual birthday parties

after that.

World Exploration

Dig up a velociraptor in Mongolia

Swim in the Caspian Sea

Make a movie in India

Care for elephants in Vietnam

Some Useful Kinds of CHARTS

People make and combine charts in lots of different ways, and sometimes even have different names for them. In fact, a few of Ana's charts in this book are combinations of the types below.
People continue to come up with new ways of showing information clearly and interestingly.

VENN DIAGRAM

Two or more overlapping circles showing what different things have in common.
You can put your interests in one circle and your friend's in the other. Try using it to compare dogs and cats, or cheeseburgers and pizza.

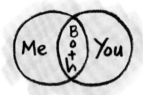

SCHEMATIC DIAGRAM

A labeled drawing that shows how something works or how it is put together.
Draw a schematic showing how to put together your favorite sandwich. Or draw a design for a robot that can do a certain chore and label each part explaining how it works.

MAP

A diagram showing where things are located.
Create a map of your home. Or draw the route you take to your friend's house, the park, or school.

COORDINATE CHART

Intersecting number lines showing the relationship between two sets of values. The bottom, or X axis, often marks something we can't change, like time or age—an "independent variable."
Ask teachers for their age group—twenty to twenty-nine, thirty to thirty-nine, and so on—and then ask how many cups of coffee they drink per day. Mark the answers with dots on a coordinate grid. Is there a correlation?

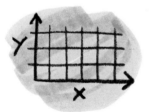

PICTOGRAM

A tally recording quantities of things in different categories.
A dot tally is a kind of pictogram. This could be a fun way to record how many classmates have zero, one, two, three, or more siblings, or how many of each class of vertebrate live at the local zoo.

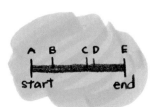

TIMELINE

A number line showing when a series of events happened.
Try a timeline for everything you've done today, or what led up to an exciting event in your life.

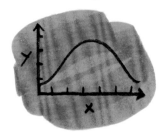

LINE CHART

A coordinate chart that has a line connecting all the data points related to one thing.
Count the students in class each day for a week. Or for one day, chart the outside temperature every hour you are in school. Is there a trend? What can you predict for the next day or week?

BAR CHART

A set of skinny rectangles whose lengths reflect different values or numbers.
At lunch, tally how many classmates eat fruit, vegetables, grain, protein, and dairy. (Kids will get counted multiple times.) Use bars to show the results. Which food groups were eaten the most?

PIES and WAFFLES and STACKED (snack?) BARS

These are all ways to show parts of a whole.
For one day, keep track of your activities and how long you spend doing each one.
You can round to the nearest hour or half-hour. Divide a circle, square, or bar into 24 hour or 48 half-hour sections, and color in.

CALENDAR

A calendar is a chart? Yes! It organizes time into weeks, months, and years.
Mark your classmates' birthdays! Schedule what you need to do on a project before its due date.

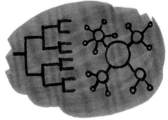

FLOW CHART or ORGANIZATIONAL CHART

A diagram dividing something into smaller or more specific parts or groups.
This can be used to consider actions and their outcomes, or to sort things into categories and subcategories. Diagram your school's authority structure, starting with the principal.

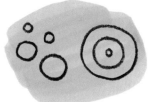

PROPORTIONAL AREA CHART

A way to compare different amounts or quantities when the differences are large.
Draw a child next to a cookie. Now draw a cookie big enough for the whole class, and then the whole school! Or, if you know the formulas for area, you can use the actual number of students in your class, school, and district. Plug these into the formula for a square or circle—as A—to find the length of a side or the radius. Now you can draw the right-sized shapes for comparison.